AMELIA
BEDELIA
GOES CAMPING

Other Avon Camelot Books by
Peggy Parish

AMELIA BEDELIA AND THE BABY
AMELIA BEDELIA HELPS OUT
GOOD WORK, AMELIA BEDELIA

By PEGGY PARISH

PICTURES BY
LYNN SWEAT

A Snuggle & Read Story Book

AVON BOOKS
A division of
The Hearst Corporation
1790 Broadway
New York, New York 10019

Published by arrangement with William Morrow & Company, Inc.
Library of Congress Catalog Card Number: 84-7979
ISBN: 0-380-70067-0
RL:1.5

The Greenwillow Books edition contains the following Library of
Congress Cataloging in Publication Data:
Parish, Peggy.
Amelia Bedelia goes camping.
Summary: As always, Amelia Bedelia follows exactly the instructions given to her
on a camping trip, including pitching a tent and rowing boats. [1. Camping—Fiction.
2. Humorous stories] I. Sweat, Lynn. ill. II. Title. III. Series.
PZ7.P219Ao 1985 [E] 84-7979

First Camelot Printing, March 1986

Printed in the U.S.A.

BAN 10 9 8 7 6 5 4 3 2 1

FOR REBECCA AND ALEX GUSHIN

WITH LOVE

AMELIA
BEDELIA
GOES CAMPING

"Hurry up, Amelia Bedelia,"
called Mr. Rogers.
"I'm coming, I'm coming,"
said Amelia Bedelia.
"Did we get everything?"
asked Mrs. Rogers.
"I would say so,"
said Amelia Bedelia.

"Good," said Mr. Rogers.

"It's time to hit the road."

"Hit the road?"

asked Amelia Bedelia.

"All right." She picked up a stick.

And Amelia Bedelia hit the road.

"Stop that!" shouted Mr. Rogers.
"Get into the car."
Amelia Bedelia got into the car.
"I'm so excited," she said.
"I've never been camping."
"You will have fun," said Mrs. Rogers.

They rode for a long time.
Finally Mr. Rogers stopped the car.
"Wake up, Amelia Bedelia,"
said Mrs. Rogers. "This is it."

Amelia Bedelia looked all around.
"But where is the camp?"
she asked.
"The camp is in the car,"
said Mr. Rogers.

"In the car!" said Amelia Bedelia.
"We're going to camp in the car?"
"The things we need
to make the camp
are in the car," said Mr. Rogers.
"Make the camp!"
said Amelia Bedelia.
"We have to make the camp?"

"Just forget it," said Mr. Rogers.
"I'll put the tent here.
We can pitch it later."
"All right," said Amelia Bedelia.

"Now let's have some fun,"
said Mr. Rogers.
"Let's catch some fish."
"I've never caught fish,"
said Amelia Bedelia.
"Is it like catching a ball?"
Mr. Rogers laughed.
"It's more fun," he said.
"I will show you how."

"Did you bring any cookies?"
asked Mrs. Rogers.
"Yes," said Amelia Bedelia.
"I made up a new kind."
Amelia Bedelia got the cookies.
"Chocolate!" said Mr. Rogers.
"My favorite."

He took a bite.
"They are so crunchy!" he said.
"That's the potato chips,"
said Amelia Bedelia.
"I do love potato chips.
I put in a whole bag.
I call them chocolate chip cookies."

Mr. and Mrs. Rogers
looked at each other.
"Call them what you like,"
said Mrs. Rogers.
"Just make them often."
"Bring them along
and follow me," said Mr. Rogers.
"Let's find a good fishing spot."

They walked along the bank.
After a bit, Mr. Rogers stopped.
He looked at the water.
"This looks good," he said.

Amelia Bedelia stopped.
"I see one! I see a fish,"
she said. "I'll catch it."
"Wait!" said Mr. Rogers.
But Mr. Rogers was too late.
Amelia Bedelia was in the water.

"Here, fishy. Here, fishy," she called.

Then she grabbed the fish.

"I caught it!" she yelled.

"What a big one!" said Mrs. Rogers.

Amelia Bedelia looked at the fish.

The fish looked at Amelia Bedelia.

"All right," said Amelia Bedelia.

"Away you go."

The fish swam away.

"Amelia Bedelia!" yelled Mr. Rogers.

"Why did you do that?"

Amelia Bedelia looked surprised.
"Why not?" she said.
"You just said to catch a fish.
I did that."
"Oh, go away," said Mr. Rogers.
"Thank you," said Amelia Bedelia.
"I am wet. I do need to change."

Amelia Bedelia started to leave.
"Oh, Amelia Bedelia,"
said Mrs. Rogers.
"Please start a fire in the grill."
"Use pine cones to start it,"
said Mr. Rogers.
"And put on some coffee."
"All right," said Amelia Bedelia.

Amelia Bedelia walked to the car.

She changed into dry clothes.

"Now," said Amelia Bedelia,

"I'll surprise Mr. Rogers.

I'll pitch that tent."

She walked over to the tent.

"Shoot," said Amelia Bedelia.

"I can't even lift it."

"Need some help?" said someone.
Amelia Bedelia turned around.
"Who are you?" she asked.
"I'm Harry," said one boy.
"I'm Mike," said the other boy.
"I'm Amelia Bedelia,"
said Amelia Bedelia.

"Amelia Bedelia!" said Harry.
"We've heard about you."
"You have!" said Amelia Bedelia.
"That's nice.
Now will you help me
pitch this tent?"
"Where do you want to pitch it?"
asked Mike.
"The big thing is to pitch it,"
said Amelia Bedelia.
"It can come down
where it wants to."
The boys grinned at each other.

“Okay, let’s do it,” said Harry.

They all caught hold of the tent.

They picked it up.

And they pitched that tent.

"Hooray!" said Amelia Bedelia.

"We did it!"

"Maybe we should pitch it again,"

said Mike.

"Why?" said Amelia Bedelia.

"It's in the bushes," said Harry.

"That's a good place for it,"
said Amelia Bedelia.
"It's out of the way."

"Hey," said Mike.

"Mom is calling us."

"Thank you for helping me,"
said Amelia Bedelia.

She watched the boys go.

"I had better get that fire started,"
said Amelia Bedelia.
She got some wood
and pine cones.
She put them in the grill.

"Live and learn,"
said Amelia Bedelia.
"I didn't know pine cones
could start a fire.
I want to see this."
Amelia Bedelia sat down.
She waited and waited.
But the fire did not start.
Suddenly she jumped up.
"The coffee!" she said.
"I forgot to put on the coffee."

She poured coffee
on the pine cones.
"Now it should start," she said.

Mr. and Mrs. Rogers walked up.
"Why isn't the fire burning?"
asked Mrs. Rogers.
"The pine cones haven't started
it yet," said Amelia Bedelia.
"Did you try using a match?"
asked Mr. Rogers.

"You didn't tell me to do that,"
said Amelia Bedelia.
"Never mind, I'll do it,"
said Mr. Rogers.
"You put on some coffee."
"I did," said Amelia Bedelia.
"Didn't I put on enough?"

"Oh, go jump in the lake,"
said Mr. Rogers.
Amelia Bedelia stamped her foot.
"I will not," she said.
"I have no more dry clothes."

Mr. Rogers laughed.

"You win," he said.

"Can you row a boat?"

"Certainly," said Amelia Bedelia.

"Use any of the boats,"

said Mr. Rogers. "Have fun."

Amelia Bedelia found the boats.
"I'll just use all of them,"
she said.

She pushed boats
this way and that.
The boats were rowed.

Amelia Bedelia went back
to Mr. and Mrs. Rogers.
"That was fun," she said.
"What is next?"
"I need the tent stakes,"
said Mr. Rogers.
"I'll get them," said Amelia Bedelia.
She ran to the car.
She brought back a package.
"Here," said Amelia Bedelia.

Mr. Rogers opened the package.

"What in tarnation!" he said.

"Didn't I cut them right?"

asked Amelia Bedelia.

"They look like tents to me."

"How am I going to pitch the tent?"
asked Mr. Rogers.
"Don't fret," said Amelia Bedelia.
"I pitched the tent."
Mr. Rogers looked.
"Where is the tent?" he asked.

"In the bushes,"
said Amelia Bedelia.
"Just where it landed."

"That does it!"

shouted Mr. Rogers.

He stamped off.

Mrs. Rogers went after him.

"Why is he so upset?"
asked Amelia Bedelia.
"I was just trying to help him."
Mr. and Mrs. Rogers came back.
"It's all right, Amelia Bedelia,"
said Mrs. Rogers.
"We can sleep under the stars."

"I'll help you get
the sleeping bags,"
said Mr. Rogers.
"I can do it," said Amelia Bedelia.
She went to the car.
Amelia Bedelia came back slowly.
She was carrying some bags.
"Shhh," she whispered.
"I think they are sleeping.
But how can you tell?"

Mr. and Mrs. Rogers stared
at Amelia Bedelia.
Then Mrs. Rogers said,
"Never mind, Amelia Bedelia."
"I'll get this camp shipshape,"
said Mr. Rogers.
"That sounds like fun,"
said Amelia Bedelia.
"What kind of ship shape
will we make?"
"You have done enough,"
said Mr. Rogers.
"I'll do this."

Amelia Bedelia walked away.
"I don't know much about camping,"
she said. "But I do know one thing.
It's time to eat."

Amelia Bedelia bustled around.

She did this and that.

Finally she had everything ready.

"Mr. and Mrs. Rogers,"
called Amelia Bedelia.
"It's time to eat."
"I'm sure ready,"
said Mrs. Rogers.
She and Mr. Rogers came.

"Fried chicken! Stuffed eggs!"
said Mr. Rogers. "What a feast!"
All three ate and ate.
"Now I'm stuffed," said Mr. Rogers.

"There's one more thing,"
said Amelia Bedelia.
"I'll go and get it."

Soon she came back singing,
"Happy birthday to you!"
"My birthday!" said Mr. Rogers.
"I forgot my birthday."
"Blow out the candles,"
said Mrs. Rogers.
"And cut the cake."
Mr. Rogers did just that.

Then he said, “Amelia Bedelia,
this is the best camping trip ever.”
Amelia Bedelia smiled.
“Let’s do it again,” she said.
“I do love camping.”

PEGGY PARISH is the author of many books enjoyed by children of all ages. For the youngest, she has written four *I Can—Can You?* books. Her easy-to-read books include nine about well-loved Amelia Bedelia (including *Amelia Bedelia and the Baby; Amelia Bedelia Helps Out; Good Work, Amelia Bedelia;* and *Teach Us, Amelia Bedelia*), *Mind Your Manners*, and *The Cats' Burglar*. For slightly older readers she has written *Key to the Treasure, Hermit Dan*, and *Let's Be Indians*. Originally from Manning, South Carolina, where she once again lives, Ms. Parish has taught school in Oklahoma, Kentucky, and New York.

LYNN SWEAT is a painter and well-known illustrator. His work has been exhibited in New York, Texas, and California. Mr. Sweat has illustrated a number of Peggy Parish's books, among them, *Amelia Bedelia and the Baby; Amelia Bedelia Helps Out; Good Work, Amelia Bedelia; Teach Us, Amelia Bedelia;* and *The Cats' Burglar*. He lives in Weston, Connecticut.